E1E10

The story of Old MacDonald, who had
a farm, with pictures by Gus Clarke.

Red Fox

For Emma, Ruth and David

A Red Fox Book

Published by Random House Children's Books
20 Vauxhall Bridge Road, London SW1V 2SA

A division of Random House UK Ltd
London Melbourne Sydney Auckland
Johannesburg and agencies throughout the world

First published in 1992 by Andersen Press Ltd

Red Fox edition 1994

Printed in Hong Kong

RANDOM HOUSE UK Limited Reg. No. 954009

ISBN 0 09 9249219

Old MacDonald had a farm,

And on that farm he had some...

Ducks

With a QUACK QUACK here and a QUACK QUACK there

Here a QUACK there a QUACK

Everywhere a QUACK QUACK

Old MacDonald had a farm,

And on that farm he had some...

And on that farm he had some...

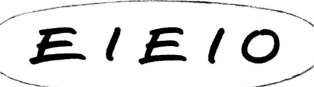

And on that farm he had some...

Hens

With a CLUCK CLUCK here   and a CLUCK CLUCK there

Here a CLUCK   there a CLUCK

Everywhere a CLUCK   CLUCK

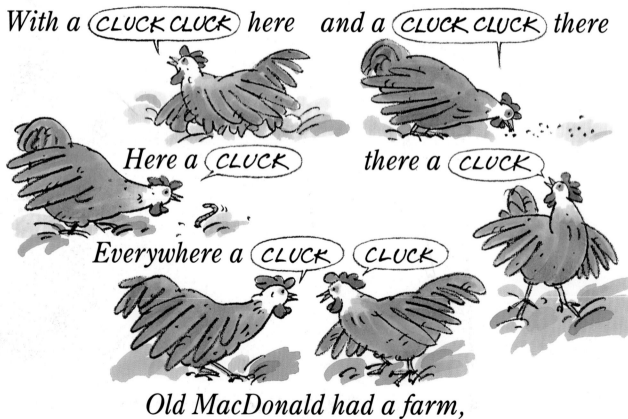

Old MacDonald had a farm,

And on that farm he had some...

And on that farm he had some...

And on that farm he had some...

Dogs

With a WOOF WOOF here and a WOOF WOOF there

Here a WOOF there a WOOF

Everywhere a WOOF WOOF

Old MacDonald had a farm,

Now, on that farm he'd had...

And now he runs a...

Camping Site

E I E I O

With a big tent here

and a little tent there

Here a tent

there a tent

Everywhere a caravan

Old MacDonald had a farm,

Some bestselling Red Fox picture books

THE BIG ALFIE AND ANNIE ROSE STORYBOOK
by Shirley Hughes
OLD BEAR
by Jane Hissey
OI! GET OFF OUR TRAIN
by John Burningham
I WANT A CAT
by Tony Ross
NOT NOW, BERNARD
by David McKee
ALL JOIN IN
by Quentin Blake
THE SAND HORSE
by Michael Foreman and Ann Turnbull
BAD BORIS GOES TO SCHOOL
by Susie Jenkin-Pearce
BILBO'S LAST SONG
by J.R.R. Tolkien
MATILDA
by Hilaire Belloc and Posy Simmonds
WILLY AND HUGH
by Anthony Browne
THE WINTER HEDGEHOG
by Ann and Reg Cartwright
A DARK, DARK TALE
by Ruth Brown
HARRY, THE DIRTY DOG
by Gene Zion and Margaret Bloy Graham
DR XARGLE'S BOOK OF EARTHLETS
by Jeanne Willis and Tony Ross
JAKE
by Deborah King